The Whitest Smile

Wilbur Morris loved being a dentist. Unfortunately no one loved him as a dentist.

Trying to accommodate patients, Wilbur stayed open late three nights a week but still barely managed to fill the time slots. Even as he offered to stay open later, his clients continued to drift away, as if they knew his practice was in dire trouble. In desperation, Wilbur offered a special half off any treatment on Friday evenings from seven to ten.

No one took him up on the offer.

You have to admit failure, Wilbur, old boy, he thought as he dragged the sandwich board notice inside from the sidewalk. He tucked it in behind the receptionist desk. The desk he no longer needed. Why bother hiring a full time receptionist when hardly anyone called?

Switching off the front light, he headed to the back, passing the two examination rooms. He paused in the doorway of each one. Instruments gleamed on the sterile trays. The drills folded neat beside the arm rests. Even the spit sinks and cups were polished. Wilbur believed in a clean, ordered office.

How could it have all gone so wrong?

He didn't overcharge. If anything, his prices were too reasonable. Below guidelines. He didn't believe in being greedy. He wanted to help people, believed he was offering excellent service at reasonable rates. He didn't understand why it wasn't working.

Maybe I shouldn't be a dentist, he thought.

Maybe his mother was right and he should have been a lawyer.

But he loved being a dentist.

He loved the bright, cleanness of sparkling teeth. He loved helping to improve people's smiles. When people had better smiles, their lives went better. They weren't afraid to talk or smile. Misunderstandings cleared away as folks originally thought of as sullen and unfriendly but only afraid of opening their mouths now spoke with confidence and connected with their neighbors. Wilbur had seen the effect, seen the confidence and happiness blossom in people who gained brighter and whiter smiles.

So why didn't they come to him?

"I'm a nice guy," he said to the empty examination room. No one contradicted him. But no one agreed either.

He switched off the lights and headed for the back to pick up his coat. How much longer could he afford to keep the office? He'd known it was a risk leaving the group practice in

Lensville to return to the city. He'd expected it to take time, to have some competition in the larger city but he hadn't expected such a complete lack of interest. Were there that many dentists here? Weren't there enough people to accommodate one more?

It certainly didn't seem that way.

As Wilbur pulled his beige overcoat from the wooden hanger, he heard the tinkle of the front door bell. Hadn't he locked the front door after bringing in the sign? He tried to remember but couldn't. It was such an automatic action, he never paid attention. The bell stopped. Had he actually heard it? Maybe it was wishful thinking.

Or maybe it was someone trying to rob the place.

There wasn't any cash but Wilbur couldn't afford to have the machines damaged. Most of them were leased and although covered by insurance, if he'd left the door open, it would void any claim. Having to pay for those machines would spell the end of his practice.

Wilbur grabbed the black umbrella from the stand by the door. A healthy whack with the heavy wooden handle might give some thief pause, he thought. And if they had a gun? Wilbur pushed that out of his mind. He had expensive dental equipment to think of.

His rubber soled shoes made no sound as he crept back along the darkened hallway. Even with the dim light from the streetlights out front, he could see well enough. Thank goodness, he'd gone for the lighter cream shade on the walls when he'd repainted the offices. It helped reflect more of the light. Unfortunately it would also help the thief.

Wilbur passed the back examination room. He paused just outside the doorway. Turn on the light or not? It would blind the thief but would also blind Wilbur as well. Maybe if he closed his eyes, then squinted. That might work. He gave himself a nod and reached for the light switch.

Even behind his closed eyelids, the light flared. He squinted, gripping the umbrella.

The room was empty. He snapped the light off again, plunging back into darkness. The front examination room lay a few paces away. Would the thief have noticed the flash of light on and off? Maybe he would think it was automated.

Wilbur might still catch him.

Gripping the umbrella tighter, he moved toward the front examination room. With each silent step, his heart thudded louder in his chest. It drowned out everything; the cars driving past on the street out front, the quiet squish of his shoes as they pressed on the white tiles. Could the thief hear his heart? It roared like thunder in Wilbur's ears. His hands trembled as he clenched the umbrella. His knees felt weak.

Replacement costs, he thought, think about the deductible.

Another step and he reached the doorway. His hand fumbled for the light. He closed his eyes.

The light flared. A howling snare sounded.

He heard the crash of an instrument tray hitting the floor, the tinkling of instruments sprayed across the tiles. His eyes squinted. He swung the umbrella.

Something hit him on the left shoulder before he could complete the swing. Wilbur stumbled and fell. Someone fell on top of him. The snarl sounded loud in his ear. He smelled the stench of decay.

Tooth decay.

A wide open mouth filled his vision. He spotted over developed canines, yellowed with excess plaque, but the worst were the obvious black holes in the back molars.

"You've got horrible cavities," Wilbur said. "And that halitosis is atrocious."

The mouth closed a little and the face drew back. A pale man with sharp features and somewhat bloodshot eyes stared at Wilbur.

"What?" he said.

"I could fill those for you," Wilbur said. "But I think you need a plague treatment first.

Probably several. When was the last time you saw a dentist?"

The man's browed furled. "I don't remember." He spoke with a thick accent that Wilbur couldn't identify.

"That's no good at all," Wilbur said. "I was closing up but I could do an initial treatment right now. Wouldn't take longer than half an hour. Maybe forty-five minutes."

The man's tongue, narrow and pink, poked out, touching the sharp canines. "What kind of initial treatment?"

"We could get rid of some of that plaque to begin with," Wilbur said. "You've got a nice set of teeth. They shouldn't be so yellow. If you'd just let me up."

And that was how Wilbur found himself bent over the man's open mouth. Even after rinsing several times with the strongest mint flavored rinse Wilbur found the man's halitosis was still strong enough to almost knock Wilbur back.

"When was the last time you flossed?" Wilbur said.

The man closed his mouth as Wilbur leaned back. "Flossed?"

The initial plaque treatment took almost an hour and a half, almost twice as long as Wilbur expected but he'd never seen a case this bad. He didn't believe in scolding patients but this was a special case.

"If you don't take care of your teeth you're going to lose them," he said. "It can cause tremendous health problems down the road and lead to either expensive implants or dentures. But they're never as good as your own teeth. I think we can save them. I'm willing to do my part but I need you to commit to brushing and flossing on a regular basis. What do you say, Mr. Valensor?"

The man sat in the chair, still wearing the dental bib around his neck. He ran his narrow, pink tongue along his teeth.

"They feel so smooth," he said. "You do good job." He nodded. "I let you live."

"That's very kind of you, Mr. Valensor," Wilbur said. "Now what about that flossing?"

"I...I don't know how."

"Let me show you."

Wilbur gave Mr. Valensor a fresh tooth-brush and three packages of floss. At the front counter, he switched on the computer to complete the billing.

"Do you have insurance?" Wilbur said.

The man shook his head. Black hair slicked back on his forehead did not move.

"I do take credit cards," Wilbur said. The printer spat out the invoice and Wilbur picked it up. He slid it across the counter and waited for the reaction.

Instead of balking, Mr. Valensor nodded. "You take cash?"

"Uh, sure."

Mr. Valensor pulled out a thin pocket book from the inside of his jacket. He counted out several fifties and finished with a twenty.

Wilbur counted it out. "I don't have any change here."

Mr. Valensor waved his hand. "You keep the change."

"Fine. Let's set up your next appointment." Wilbur opened the appointment calendar on the computer. "I can see you Tuesday at eleven in the morning."

"No daytime appointments," the man said. "Only evening. Late."

"Um, okay. How about next Wednesday at eight?"

"It will be dark then?"

"Yes."

The man nodded. "I'll take it."

Wilbur filled out an appointment card and handed it to Mr. Valensor. As he plucked it from Wilbur's fingers, Wilbur noticed the long, thin nails on Mr. Valensor's hand. He'd never seen a man with nails like that but he made no sign of it. Wilbur didn't judge. He believed in live and let live.

Mr. Valensor headed for the door, then turned just before he reached it.

"You are a good dentist," he said. "I will recommend you to my friends."

"Please do," Wilbur said.

He blinked and the door was swinging shut. Mr. Valensor had vanished. This time Wilbur did remember to lock the front door. He couldn't trust that every thief would turn out to need dental work and be distracted by it.

Little did Wilbur know that he had just saved his practice.

The days still passed with few patients, but by late afternoon the phone began to ring. Men and women with strange accents or deep, gravelly voices asked for evening appointments. Within a few days, Wilbur had filled all of his evenings for two weeks. He tried to talk them into daytime appointments but they all insisted on evenings. The clamor for evening appointments forced him to extend his evening hours. He decided to close in the mornings, letting himself sleep in. Since he had few daytime patients, it didn't matter.

When he asked how they'd heard of him, every one of them mentioned Mr. Valensor.

Wilbur had never been so glad of almost being robbed in his life.

The one thing he did notice about all his new patients was the pallor of their skin and every one of them had the worst halitosis and a terrible build up of plaque. They all confessed to not having seen a dentist for years. Centuries, insisted Mr. Belaossa although he said it with such dramatic flare Wilbur knew he was joking.

They all insisted on paying in cash, pealing off fifties and twenties, never asking for change. Before Wilbur knew it, he was having to make night deposits. He'd never had to make night deposits before. The thought of it made him giddy.

His practice was becoming successful. He'd found his niche.

Then she walked in.

'Mianna Travosa' her appointment card read. Wilbur remembered her voice when she gave her name in a deep, slow whisper. Her skin was as pale as the others but seemed to glow against her long black hair and her black dress. Eyes so dark they appeared black stared at him without blinking. Her face was a multitude of angles, high cheekbones and a slim jawline but rounded enough to be feminine. He held out his hand to show her to the back examination room. Her fingers slipped into his hand and the shock of her cool flesh sent a shiver across his shoulder. Her long pointed nails were painted a deep, dark red.

As she lifted her skirt to sit in the chair, Wilbur hurried to stand behind the head rest, out of her range of vision. His pants felt suddenly tight. How horribly unprofessional of him. He'd never had such a reaction to a patient. He hurried to the sink and turned the water on cold. Dousing his hands, he soaped up and scrubbed the skin hard. After a moment with the freezing water, he felt less restricted and more calm.

He returned to her side and slipped the bib around her neck, managing to avoid more than a passing glance at the way the neckline of her dress plunged down to reveal the swell of her breasts. He clipped the bib in place. She tilted her head, a slight smile curving her full, red lips as if she knew where he'd been looking. Of course, she was a beautiful woman and was used to such attention.

Wilbur blushed as he pulled his mask up onto his face. He was never more glad of having to wear a face mask. He hit the button on the chair and adjusted it down. She lay prone before him, her long fingered hands folded in her lap.

"Please open wide," Wilbur said.

Her halitosis was as bad as the others but the plaque build up was less. From his initial examination, he didn't see any cavities but x-rays might show some smaller ones. Best to catch them early, he always thought. Like all of Mr. Valensor's friends, her canines were quite well developed, sharpened into a point. He completed the initial exam.

"I'd like to take some x-rays," he said. "I don't see any major problems but it's always good to get a baseline. Then I'll get rid of some of that plaque and we can get that halitosis taken care of."

She bowed her head. One hand came up to touch her lips.

"Is my breath that bad?" Her deep voice almost purred the words.

His legs felt weak. Thank goodness he was sitting down.

"It's nothing we can't take care of," he said. "Regular brushing and flossing should clear that up before you know it. If it doesn't, then we can start looking at other options. But let's start with the x-rays."

He placed the lead lined cover over her body and then adjusted the x-ray beside her right jaw. As he retreated behind the partition, he was grateful for another moment to shift in his pants. They felt restrictive and he wondered if he'd be able to get away with washing his hands in freezing water again. Maybe he should get an ice pack and put it in his front pants pocket.

Get a hold of yourself, Wilbur, he thought. So she was a pretty girl. He was a professional and he had to act like it. She was a patient who needed his help and expertise. Best to keep that at the front of his mind.

The brief respite behind the partition helped him regain his equilibrium when he returned to her side. As he removed the cards from her teeth, her tongue flicked out, licking her lush lips. The tip of it caught his index finger. He felt a shock of electricity race up his finger and arm and head straight to his groin. He forced himself to sit down and take measured breaths.

"Now let's get rid of that plaque, shall we?" he said.

She hummed an agreement. Her throat quivered. He fixated on the smooth paleness of the skin at the base of her throat and along her clavicle. Her head turned toward him. The cool heat of her gaze pressured him to turn his head, just a little, just tilt it so, a little more. The smoothness of her lips brushed the side of his neck, sending another electric shock straight to his groin. He barely managed to stop a groan from escaping his mouth. Her lips pressed against his neck then he felt the cold smoothness of her teeth…

"Mianna!"

Her mouth was gone. Wilbur blinked in surprise. What?

Mr. Valensor stood in the doorway. His white hands curled into fists. His thin frame shook with fury.

"What do you think you're doing?"

Wilbur pulled the corner of his white lab coat over his lap. "I… ah was getting ready to clean her teeth."

Mr. Valensor ignored him and stepped to the other side of the dental chair. "Well?"

"I'm sorry, Boris, he is so warm…"

Mr. Valensor grabbed her arm and yanked her out of the chair. Mianna stumbled before she regained her feet as Mr. Valensor dragged her toward the door.

"Please excuse her," he said. "She is young and stupid. She doesn't understand necessities. You will be compensated for your time, doctor."

"But… her teeth…" Wilbur hurried after them. He reached the front room to find a stack of money piled on the counter and the door swinging shut.

He hadn't even had a chance to finish her cleaning.

He wanted to go after them but he couldn't leave the office open, not with money spread across the counter. He scooped it up without counting and added it to the deposit box. Originally he'd been planning to make a deposit tonight after this final appointment but now he didn't feel like it. He locked the box in the safe under the desk and went to clean up the examination room.

Even under the lingering stench of her

halitosis, he could smell the musky undercurrent of her body in the chair. He touched the plastic. It felt cool, like her skin, as if her body left no heat behind.

He sat in his chair to arrange the instruments and found himself leaning over the chair again, as if looking at her slim neck and feeling the cool smoothness of her lips on his neck. Only the uncomfortable constriction of his pants brought him out of it.

For heaven's sake, Wilbur, he thought. You're a dentist. You should be ashamed.

He forced himself to keep thinking that even as the memory of her soft lips haunted him through all the tidying up and all the way home until he forced himself to take a cold shower at one am to banish the thoughts of what he wanted to do to her.

S oon Wilbur found he needed to hire help again. Most receptionists would not work past six o'clock and as his practice continued to grow in the evening hours, such reluctance made him more and more impatient. He was willing to pay top dollar but as soon as six hit, most help was out the door. By offering overtime, he was able to get one receptionist to stay to eight o'clock three nights a week but after the second week, she abruptly quit, saying something about the creepy patients and nightmares.

Wilbur found himself alone again.

He dismissed the receptionist's natter-ings about nightmares. What did that have to do with work? Never mind that he found himself waking up at three am in a cold sweat on a regular basis, his mind filled with vague images of blood and terror. As he lay back on his clammy sheets, he invariably thought of Mianna and the press of her cool lips against his neck. At least in the privacy of his bedroom he could relieve himself but it did nothing to stop the images from filling his mind. His desire remained unfulfilled.

So Wilbur threw himself into work, and his practice thrived.

Now he found it not worth opening until three o'clock. That gave him time to get ready for the evening appointments. He stayed open later and later, to accommodate more of his evening patients. One particularly nasty molar forced him to stay open until almost midnight. With each passing moment, the man in the chair seemed to inflate with energy. His normal white pallor becoming an almost regular pink. It must be the lights, Wilbur thought. It couldn't have anything to do with the time.

That man, Reynaldo Broisa, tipped Wilbur most generously that night. Although Wilbur appreciated it, he was left with the same feeling of disappointment that haunted him every night.

Every night since Mianna.

She never returned for an appointment and Wilbur knew she needed help. Aside from his fevered dreams, it was the only motive he would admit to in the light of day, or the twilight of evening. Although the plaque build up hadn't been as bad on her teeth, she needed to get it removed and needed to have that halitosis dealt with. As a self-respecting dentist, Wilbur wouldn't have it any other way.

But she did not return. Finally, at Mr. Valensor's next checkup, Wilbur could contain himself no longer.

He handed Mr. Valensor the small cup to rinse. As Mr. Valensor swished water in his mouth and turned to spit in the sink, Wilbur pulled the mask down from his face.

"Mr. Valensor, I was wondering about one of your friends," he said.

Mr. Valensor dabbed his mouth with the edge of his paper bib. "Oh?"

Wilbur took the paper cup from the man's hand and tossed it in the waste basket by the door.

"Yes, I was concerned because I wasn't able to finish the plaque cleaning."

Mr. Valensor's eye brows drew together as he frowned. "Ah."

"Yes," Wilbur said. He suddenly felt nervous under Mr. Valensor's cold stare. His stomach twisted. Sweat trickled down his back. Stop it, he thought, he was only concerned about a patient. Her teeth and health were most important.

Squaring his shoulders, Wilbur faced Mr. Valensor's stare. "Yes, Ms. Travosa needs to have that plaque taken care of," he said. "If not by me, then by another dentist."

"But you would prefer if it were you," Mr. Valensor said.

Wilbur felt his cheeks burn. "Mr. Valensor, I am a dentist. My concern is for my patients and the welfare of their teeth."

"Of course, of course," Mr. Valensor said. "Do not trouble yourself with Ms. Travosa. She will be taken care of."

He yanked the bib from around his neck and climbed out of the chair. Without waiting for Wilbur, he headed back down the hall toward the front of reception area. Wilbur scrambled to catch up. At the front desk, Mr. Valensor stood peeling off fifties to cover the bill.

"What do you mean she'll be taken care of?" Wilbur said.

Mr. Valensor placed the money on the counter and slid it across. His dark eyes seemed to glow with intensity.

"It is none of your concern," he said. "Good night, doctor."

He stared at Wilbur for a moment then turned and left. The door swung closed behind him in its regular slow motion fashion. Wilbur hurried forward and caught the edge before it clicked shut. Before he realized what he was doing, no, before he could talk himself out of it, he stepped outside. The cool evening breeze ruffled his white coat. He locked the door and slipped the keys into his pocket.

Mr. Valensor had headed west but already Wilbur couldn't see him. No, wait, there, several blocks away he saw a figure drifting in and out of the shadows. That had to be Mr. Valensor. No one else was on the street at ten thirty.

Wilbur wrapped his coat around his body and hurried after the man. What exactly he was doing, he didn't allow himself to consider. He just had to make sure that Mianna's teeth were looked after.

The thought of her set his heart pounding. He slowed down, allowing more distance between himself and Mr. Valensor. Certainly the man wouldn't be able to hear Wilbur's heart pounding from this distance but why take the chance?

He kept pace with the figure, cutting across streets against lights if necessary. The minimal traffic in this neighborhood at night posed little problem. Wilbur had his office in a busy downtown location that thrived during the business hours but became deserted after dark. Wilbur's footsteps were the only ones he heard. Wilbur's shadow the only one he saw except for the distant figure ahead of him.

The figure turned north.

Wilbur followed.

A greater darkness stretched across the west side of street as Wilbur headed north. Even here on the east side, the building lights were few and scattered. What was it across the street with no lights? Then he saw the double wide driveway leading in and remembered.

The cemetery.

Wilbur watched as the figure ahead of him crossed the street and walked along the driveway into the cemetery. Within moments, the figure disappeared into the deeper darkness.

Wilbur waited for a lone car to drive past before he crossed the street. He reached the driveway and began to walk into the cemetery. He made it past the gates before his feet just stopped.

What are you doing, Wilbur, he thought. Without any lights, he could end up lost in the cemetery until morning, stumbling across graves and flower arrangements. Who knew who was lurking in there? Probably some homeless people who wouldn't think anything of beating him up and leaving him there. He should go back to his office and close up for the night. Head home to his lake front condo.

His empty lake front condo.

It was always empty. Wilbur didn't have

many friends. Work took up all of his time, especially now with all of the evening appointments. He had no time for socializing, even if anyone did call him.

Which they never did.

No one ever showed the slightest interest in Wilbur Morris. Except…

Mianna.

His feet started moving again and carried him all the way into the cemetery.

When he passed the mile mark he started to hear voices whispering on the breeze. Or maybe it was homeless men waiting to jump on him. His feet slowed. Maybe it was just the trees rustling, their leaves rubbing and sliding against each other. Rubbing and sliding made him think of Mianna again.

His feet moved forward.

The pavement curved to the left but Wilbur continued straight, stepping onto the grass.

It crunched beneath his feet. He felt a gentle sloop moving downward. In the distance, he heard the burble of water flowing in a creek. Over the sound, he heard voices again, closer, off to his right. He crept forward, aware it could still be the faceless homeless people that he feared.

The night was not nearly as black as he'd expected. Ambient light from the surrounding area reflected down from the overcast clouds above. He could make out dark lumps rising from the ground. Tombstones, he realized and then remembered what he was walking on.

Or who.

His shoulders hunched as he pressed his arms to his sides. What the hell was he doing out here in the middle of the night walking over peoples' graves? Had he lost his mind? He looked around and realized he didn't know exactly where he was. Oh great, Wilbur, he thought. How was he going to find the street again?

The voices ahead of him increased in volume. Some kind of argument was going on. His feet started moving again without his permission. Over a slight rise, he thought he saw figures standing in the middle of a cropping of tombstones. Wilbur hunched down behind a large square marker.

"...dangerous to all of us." The words floated on the air. Wilbur thought he recognized the voice. Could it be Mr. Valensor?

"Is it not my fault," a woman's voice said.

"You are always too impetuous. When will you learn patience?"

"I've had enough of your patience!"

The voice rose to a shout at the end of the sentence, causing Wilbur to hold his breath. He recognized that voice. Mianna!

Growls sounded.

"Not all of us think as you do, Boris!" she said.

The growls grew louder. Then Wilbur heard the sound of something striking out and the thud of a body on the ground. He jumped up and ran forward.

In the center of a circle of tombstones, Mianna lay on the ground, her hand at her throat. Mr. Valensor bent over her, his head buried in her neck. Without thinking, Wilbur leapt on his back.

"Get off her!"

Mr. Valensor reared up, flexing his shoulders. Wilbur found himself flying backward. He landed against a tombstone and fell in a heap at its base. The wind knocked out of him, he gasped for air. He grabbed the tombstone and started to pull himself to his feet. A steel vice wrapped around his neck, tightening. He gagged, twisting to look. Mr. Valensor's face filled his vision, expression twisted in anger into something horrible. Wilbur remembered it from that first night.

That first night...

"Stop it, Boris!" "Stop, look who it is!" "It's Doctor Morris."

The voices floated around him, soon drowned out by the pounding of his heart and the roaring of blood in his ears. He tried to suck in air, his mouth gaping like a fish, but nothing came. The vice grip of Mr. Valensor's hand stopped any air. Wilbur's fingers pried and pounded but nothing moved that hand. Finally the voices blurred into a loud buzzing.

He crumpled to the ground. The vice on his neck was gone. Wilbur sucked in air as fast as he could. Soon the roaring of his blood faded. His heart slowed. His neck hurt from Mr. Valensor's grip. Wilbur rubbed at it as he struggled to his feet.

In front of him, Mr. Valensor stood in the middle of a crowd of other people. His fists clenched as he glared back at Wilbur. Beyond him, Wilbur could see Mianna, standing with a hand to her throat. Her pale skin looked luminescent in the darkness, her dark hair a suggestion across her shoulders.

"How did you get here?" Mr. Valensor said.

"He followed you, of course," said Reynaldo Broisa. "You were careless, Boris."

"I am not careless."

"Obviously you are or the dentist would not be here." Reynaldo stepped between them. "It is a shame you are here, Dr. Morris. You should not have found out about us."

Wilbur tried to speak. His sore throat ached. He swallowed then tried again. "You mean found out you're vampires?"

A hush settled on the entire group. He felt their attention rivet onto him with laser focus. He almost took a step back. His foot actually moved before he noticed and stood firm. He couldn't show fear, even as his bowels clenched.

This was what a mouse must feel like cornered by a cat, he thought.

"You think I don't know what you are?" he said. His voice almost squeaked. "It wasn't hard to guess. Wanting appointments after dark, the bad halitosis. I'm not as stupid as you think I am."

"Stupid enough to have followed me." Mr. Valensor stepped forward. The others followed, encircling Wilbur. He began to shiver in the cold. He wasn't afraid, no, he wasn't. Well, maybe terrified.

"So he knows about us." Mianna stepped in front of Mr. Valensor and faced him. The breeze brought the faint musky scent of her body to Wilbur. He inhaled deep.

"He hasn't said anything to anyone, has he?" she said. "He continues to treat us, to help us. Even when he knew. Reynaldo, did he not work on your molars?"

Reynaldo nodded.

"Jasmine, did he not consult on your overbite and give you exercises for your jaw?"

A blond woman on Mianna's left bowed her head in acknowledgement.

"Then do we not owe him to hear him out?" Mianna said. She stepped back, turning toward Wilbur, her hand beckoning him to continue. But Wilbur didn't know what else to say. He knew about them, that was the only thing he'd thought of to mention. He'd always known, from the first day Mr. Valensor had broken into his office. Offering to fix the man's teeth was the only way Wilbur could think of to save his life. Then fixing the others just seemed to flow from there.

"I was afraid not to do it at first," he said. "I thought you would kill me. But then I saw you had problems with your teeth, all the plaque build up, the receding gum lines, the cavities. You need a good dentist just like anyone. I took a vow to help people in need with their teeth. I've done my best for you."

Around him, he felt the intensity of their gaze shift. Dark shadows nodded in agreement but Mr. Valensor scowled.

"He cannot learn about us and live. That is the code."

"Damn your code," Mianna said. "We have to adapt to survive."

"Your adaptations would destroy us!" Mr.

Valensor's arm blurred as he struck out at Mianna. She leapt back, his fists passing within a hair's width of her cheek. Mr. Valensor snarled and leapt forward, aiming past Mianna and toward Wilbur.

Wilbur stumbled back, feeling Mr. Valensor's claws rack across his chest. His shirt shredded. Blood beaded on his skin.

Mianna shrieked as she knocked Mr. Valensor aside.

"Run, Wilbur!"

Wilbur staggered to his feet and ran. The grass felt soft and wet under his feet. He slid as much as he ran. In the distance, he saw street-lights and headed for them. Nothing followed, nothing he could hear but he felt a creeping presence flying toward him. His shoulder blades tightened, clenching his back muscles. Rancid breath warmed the back of his neck. He ducked his head, feeling the air move over his hair as if someone had swiped at it.

A howl of rage bellowed out, followed by

a different snarl of anger. Something thudded behind him and a cacophony of growls began. A woman's voice cried out.

It sounded like Mianna.

Wilbur wanted to look back, wanted to stop but he couldn't, knew if he did he'd be dead. She given him this gift, a chance to save his life. He didn't have any right to waste it.

He kept running and didn't look back.

His feet smacked on the pavement and the solid footing gave him an extra burst of speed. He raced into the street, not bothering with the light (red) or the crosswalk (dark) and kept going. As he reached the corner and turned east, he heard other footsteps following.

Coming up fast.

Wilbur pushed harder. His lungs burned as he gulped for air. A painful stitch pierced his right side. His heart pounded so fast he thought it would burst through his back and he'd leave it lying on the sidewalk behind him.

The dark storefronts blurred beside him.

Ahead he saw the sign for Tony's Pizza Emporium, just three stores before his office. He raced past. His fingers fumbled in his pocket.

He had the key out as he slid up to the door. The footsteps following pounded past Tony's. Wilbur jammed the key in the lock and yanked the door open.

Three running steps carried him through the reception area to the back hallway. He bypassed the first examination room and headed for the second one. A moment later, the pounding footsteps followed him down the hallway.

The light sprang on in the room. The flash of it blinded Wilbur. He clenched the drill and held it in front of him as he blinked. He felt a presence sweep across the room.

"Boris!" Mianna's scream came from the reception area.

A snarl filled Wilbur's ears. The stench of Mr. Valensor's breath filled Wilbur's face. Not as bad as before, Wilbur thought. His eyes cleared to show him Mr. Valensor's sharp canines, ready to bite.

Wilbur shoved the drill forward.

He grabbed Mr. Valensor's collar and pressed the button. The drill whined. The cloying stench of burning porcelain filled Wilbur's nostrils.

Mr. Valensor shrieked and tried to pull away but Wilbur hung on. The vampire twisted his head, dislodging the drill, but not before Wilbur saw the hole burned into his left incisor.

As the vampire howled, Wilbur grabbed a sample tube from the counter. He cut the top and shoved it into the vampire's mouth. He squeezed hard, sending the clear goo into Mr. Valensor's mouth. Mr. Valensor's hands grabbed Wilbur. His nails dug in, piercing Wilbur's skin. Wilbur hissed but held on to the tube until it finished. Mr. Valensor shoved and Wilbur flew back. He hit the wall and slid down to the floor.

He heard Mr. Valensor coughing, trying to clear his mouth.

Mianna appeared in the doorway. She took a step toward Wilbur.

"Don't let him," Wilbur said. "Keep his mouth shut."

Mianna fell on Mr. Valensor. She grabbed him from behind, trapping his arms to his sides. A gurgle of rage sounded. The vampire twisted, trying to escape but she held on. After five minutes, Wilbur signaled her to let him go.

Mr. Valensor fell to his knees when Mianna released him. His hands dug at his mouth but the goo had hardened, fixing Mr. Valensor's open mouthed snarled for eternity.

"It's brand new," Wilbur said. "The latest in dental fixatives. They're testing it to see if it will replace implants. Personally, I think it's too dangerous. What do you think?"

Mr. Valensor lunged for him again but Wilbur retreated behind the chair, out of reach.

Reynaldo and Jasmine entered and grabbed Mr. Valensor's arms.

"It's time to change, Boris," Mianna said. "We can't just go around killing everyone anymore. We want good dental benefits just like anyone else."

Mr. Valensor gurgled response and flailing arms gave his answer. Mianna nodded to the others. Reynaldo and Jasmine began to drag Mr. Valensor away.

"Reynaldo, I'll want to check that molar in a couple of weeks," Wilbur said.

The big vampire nodded. "I'll make an appointment, doctor."

They hauled Mr. Valensor away. Wilbur heard the front door click shut behind them.

"I apologize for Boris," Mianna said. "And for myself. I was... inappropriate at my last appointment."

"Um, that's all right," Wilbur said.

"I just..." She stepped forward. Her thin hand trailed down his bicep. "I've always been attracted to dentists."

Wilbur swallowed in a dry mouth. "Really?"
She nodded.

"Maybe we can go for a drink sometime," Wilbur said. "But you really need to have that plaque taken care of."

She smiled but her lips remained closed.

"If you got rid of that plaque, you could smile more openly," he said. "I could even give you a whitening treatment."

"You would do that? For me? After everything?"

"Sure," he said. "You need good tooth care too."

This time her smile was larger. She leaned forward and kissed his cheek. The sensual musk of her was drowned out by the rotting stench of her breath.

"Have a seat," Wilbur said. "I've got an extra coat in the closet. Let's get started on those teeth."

Wilbur splashed water on this face and dabbed away the blood from his chest. The clock told him it was already after twelve but he wanted to get started on Mianna's teeth right away. She deserved the best treatment he could give her and the sooner he started the better.

After all, he couldn't wait to have a drink with her.

Wilbur pulled up his mask and bent over Mianna.

"Now open wide," he said.

And she did.

About the Author

Based in Toronto, Canada, Rebecca M. Senese writes horror, science fiction and mystery/crime, often all at once in the same story. Garnering an Honorable Mention in "The Year's Best Science Fiction" and nominated for numerous Aurora Awards, her work has appeared in *Tesseracts 16: Parnassus Unbound, Imaginarium 2012, Tesseracts 15: A Case of Quite Curious Tales, Ride the Moon, TransVersions, Deadbolt Magazine, On Spec, The Vampire's Crypt, Storyteller, Reflection's Edge, Future Syndicate* and *Into the Darkness,* amongst others.

When not serving up tales of the macabre, mysterious or wondrous, she volunteers as a zombie or vampire at haunted attractions in October to stalk and scare all the unsuspecting innocents.

Find Me Online

Website - http://www.RebeccaSenese.com
Twitter - http://twitter.com/RebeccaSenese

Printed in Great Britain
by Amazon.co.uk, Ltd.,
Marston Gate.